I0517092

Wild Journey

Alysa Marcial

ISBN-13:
978-0692154229
ISBN-10:
0692154221

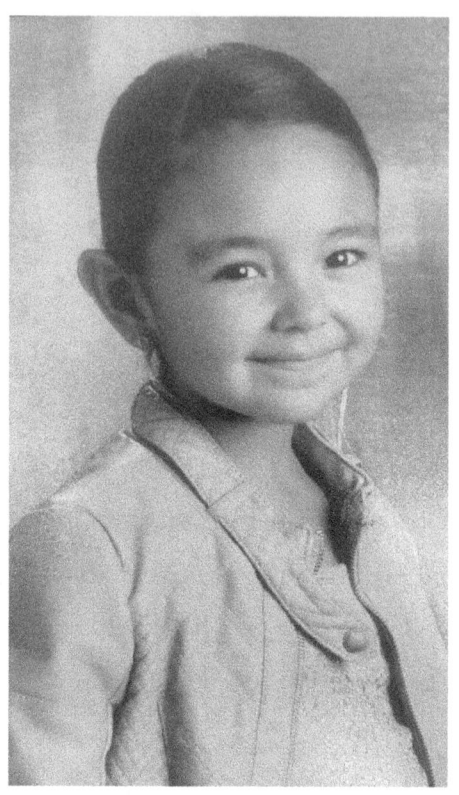

My name is Alysa Cruz Marcial Rivera. I am ten years old and going into the fifth grade. My favorite hobby is riding horses. My love for all animals is what inspired me to write this book. I plan to be a veterinarian when I grow up. I hope you enjoy my book.

This book is dedicated to my family. To my Mom and Dad for making sure I got to my writing sessions. I also thank Mr. David Chappell for being an amazing teacher. I couldn't have completed this book without you.

Literary Legacies

This book is brought to you with the help of the nonprofit Literary Legacies. Founded by author David Chappell, Literary Legacies guides students grades 4-12, word by word, how to write their own fiction or nonfiction book. Literary Legacies hopes to inspire youth to find healing, strength, confidence, agency, and purpose through the power of writing. If you would like to learn more about this nonprofit, please visit literarylegacies.org

Chapter One

"Oh, I love the summer!" Stella says to her siblings as they start to leave the wolves' den.

Aaron asks, "What do you guys want to do during the hunt today?" Stella does not know why he even asked, because Link always decides for them.

Link says, "Today let's not play a game, let's wrestle."

Stella responds, "Mom and Dad say we need to stop wrestling."

"Who said that they are going to know?" Link responds nastily.

Link proceeds to start walking out of the den saying, "Come on everyone." As he leads them out into the forest, he says to his siblings, "We should go far away so Mom and Dad can't catch us when they get back."

Stella, Star, and Aaron all give in to his demands. Stella says, "Okay big brother. We will do what you say."

Stella walks happily with her siblings, enjoying the warm Alaskan day. The birds are chirping, and the sun is shining through the trees.

After walking for quite some time, they come to a clearing in the woods. Link says to them, "Let's stop here." The four siblings run into the middle of the grass patch and start to wrestle.

Star says to them, "Let's pick a partner to wrestle. I pick Link!"

Aaron says, "I was hoping that you would pick Link. I love wrestling with my little sister!"

Stella responds, "I love wrestling with you Aaron because I am small, and I can run through your legs."

The two pairs start to wrestle, and they are having a fantastic, fun time. But, they are completely unaware of their surroundings.

6

Aaron suddenly stops playing when he hears a large twig break in the bushes nearby. He puts his nose in the air and smells intently.

Stella asks him, "What's wrong brother?"

"I need you to get over behind those trees."

"No, I don't want to!" she responds.

"Now!" Aaron pushes her forcefully into the forest behind several trees.

After Stella is out of sight, the creature that was causing the noise comes out of the bushes. With a large roar, a twelve-foot grizzly bear emerges and charges the three wolf pups.

Aaron screams, "RUN!!!"

Link and Star turn to see why Aaron is yelling, and they see the large grizzly approaching. The three start to run as fast as they can. Stella is watching from behind the tree shaking in fear. She waits there for several minutes before she starts to run back toward the den. In the distance, she hears the howling screams

of her siblings with her keen wolf ears. She begins to

sob as she runs the several miles back to her den.

Chapter Two

She arrives back at the den, out of breath from her terrified run. She hides in the back of the den until the rest of the pack arrives home. About twenty minutes later, the pack arrives. Her parents see her hiding in the back of the den by herself. Hunter, her father and pack leader, says to her, "Where are your siblings? Link was supposed to keep you all together."

Moon, her mother, asks "Why are you crying? What happened?"

Stella looks up at them with tears in her eyes. She sobbed, "I'm so sorry, but Link wanted us to wrestle, so we went far far away so we would not get caught. When we were wrestling, Aaron heard something and pushed me into the forest. Right after he did that, a giant grizzly bear attacked the other three. I was too scared to move for a long time, but then I started to run home. I could hear their screams in the distance. The bear killed them!"

Moon gasps! "Why did you all go so far?!" Tears spill out of her eyes knowing that her other three pups are dead.

Hunter says sorrowfully, "Why couldn't you four have just stayed here!"

Both of Stella's parents come into the den to console her. Other wolves come into the den and hear the crying and Hunter tells the wolf pack that three of his pups, and the two heirs to the throne, have been killed. The entire pack is devastated.

Hunter tells Stella that night after the pack mourns the death of her siblings that they caught a few rabbits for dinner and one caribou.

Chapter Three

Six months later... Stella is ten months old and growing into a strong and confident wolf. Over the past six months, several pups have been born in the wolf pack. It was a particularly cold and snowy winter in Alaska that year. The deer, moose, and caribou were plentiful. The wolf pack was well fed.

Stella leaves the den one morning wanting to explore the forest. After she is in the forest for several hours, she smells a wolf coming toward her. She recognizes the scent and when Chance came out of the tree line, she smiles and walks toward him. Chance walks up to Stella and says, "Hi Stella! I could smell you a long way away and wanted to see what you were doing."

"I was just coming into the woods to look around. This is the first time I have been out by myself since my siblings passed away."

"You don't have to be afraid anymore. I am here for you. I am a grown wolf now."

"Chance, do you want to walk with me?" Stella wants to know.

"I will absolutely love to," he answers.

"Umm, you sure?"

"Wow! Chance is really cute!" Stella said to herself as they walked. She continued thinking to herself, "I would love to have a family of my own with him."

Chapter Four

Stella and Chance are near the den and the older wolves are heading out. Stella has been feeling more confident in the last few weeks since walking with Chance in the woods. As their parents and the adults left the den, she turns to Chance and asks him, "Do you want to play hide-and-go-seek near the den?"

"Sure, that sounds like fun!"

They play hide-and-go-seek for quite some time and they are both wondering why the parents are taking so much time. Stella says to Chance, "What is taking them so long? I hope nothing happened."

"They probably got a big kill and it's taking them a long time to drag it home. Don't worry Stella, everything is going to be okay."

Thirty minutes later, they hear the faint noises of the pack arriving. The closer they get, the more the noises start to sound like crying. The pack is moaning and crying tears as they arrive at the den. All of the pups come out to the den's entrance to greet the parents. The pups are all asking, "What's wrong?"

Stella is looking around the returning pack for her parents to ask them what happened on the hunt. She keeps looking and looking, but she is not finding them. Stella asks one of the adults named Ace what happened, saying, "Ace, Ace, what happened? Why is everyone crying? Where are my parents?"

"Wait here young one, the Elders are coming to talk to you."

The Elders come into the den and they ask Stella to come with them out of view of the rest of the pack. When they take her away from the den, they circle around her. Stella is feeling anxious to know what happened. The most senior Elder, Loki, speaks to Stella, "I am sorry to have to tell you this young Stella, but your parents were killed by the weapons of the humans. We did not see them coming. Their weapons rang out in the distance and struck many of us. Your parents were leading the pack, so they were hit first and did not survive the attack."

Stella immediately begins to cry and howl as loud as she can. The rest of the pack by now has heard the bad news. They hear Stella howling and they all rush over to console her. She is shaking, and sobbing, because now she is all alone in the world with no family to support her. She thought in that instant, "I am all alone. What am I going to do without my family to support and protect me?"

Midnight, Chance's father and second-in-command, comes up to the pack Elders and says, "This is a tragic loss for our pack. We must think about what we will do going forward. As second-in-command, I order a pack meeting tomorrow morning."

Loki responds to Midnight saying, "Yes, we will have the meeting tomorrow. Everyone try your best to get some sleep. This was a very hard night. Stella, come with me to my den and we will talk."

Loki and Stella head back to Loki's den. Stella is still in tears mourning the loss of her parents. When they arrive at the den, Loki pulls Stella close to him. "All will be okay young pup. I promise to protect you with my life. I may be old in age, but I have a little bit of fight left in me. Nothing will happen to you as long as I am living. I swear that on your father's grave."

Stella, with tears still streaming down her face, turns to Loki and says, "Thank you Elder Loki. In this time of grief, you have stilled my heart at least a little bit. Thank you for letting me sleep here with you tonight. I did not want to sleep in my den by myself with the memories of my dead family looming over me."

Stella and Loki lie down and spend the night talking

about the memories of her parents until she falls asleep.

Chapter Five

The next morning arrives and Stella and Loki wake up to the sounds of the pack walking around the woods. Midnight announces to the pack, "It is time for the convening of the pack meeting!" Loki and Stella go to the pack meeting area with the rest of the wolves. Midnight calls the meeting to order. "Pack, we are here today to discuss serious business. We must elect a new leader to head the pack going forward. Young Stella is too young to take over for her parents. I nominate myself as second-in-command. I have been second-in-command for the past ten years and I am ready to take over the pack. Are there any other candidates?" There was silence from the pack and the Elders called a formal vote.

Loki says, "Elders, vote for your approval." The Elders all spoke and voted to have Midnight as their next pack leader.

After the vote, Midnight responds saying, "Thank you Elders and thank you pack, I will be the best leader the pack has ever had." Stella looks at him sideways, because her father had just passed, and she thought that he was a the best pack leader ever!

Chapter Six

The pack goes out for an early morning hunt for breakfast. Stella and Chance hang back around the den to spend some more time with each other. They are starting to really have feelings for each other. They are walking through the woods when the older wolves come running back to the den, out of breath. When the entire pack arrives, Midnight calls for a meeting in order to discuss what happened during the hunt with the entire pack.

The meeting is called for that night and when night time arrives, Stella and Loki walk to the meeting to see what Midnight has to say. Midnight stands on the pack leader rock and says to the pack, "We had another incident with the human killers today. They attacked us with their weapons and thankfully none of us were hurt this time. There is something wrong in the pack that is making us unlucky. I know what it is…" There was a pause, and Midnight turns and looks at Stella. "Tragedy has come to the Hunter bloodline. All except one of his children, his wife, and even he, has been killed. His bloodline is bad luck. As long as Stella is here, we will continue to find our pack under threat."

Loki speaks up, "Stella is not bad luck! Neither is her bloodline! Bad things happen to good wolves."

Midnight responds, "I do not care what you say old wolf! Stella is bad for us. I hereby decree that she is banished from the pack for the rest of her life."

Loki says, "I have sworn an oath to protect Stella with my life. If you think you are going to banish her to the wilderness, I am here to tell you that I will not allow it."

Midnight responds, "Does that mean you are challenging my order Loki? You know that is punishable by death."

"I will not let you do this. Try your best to defeat me, but my honor will destroy you Midnight."

Midnight growls loudly and jumps after Loki. The fight between Midnight and Loki is brutal. They bite and claw at each other for several minutes. Loki moves for a death bite on Midnight but misses and exposes the back of his neck. Midnight sees the opening and bites down on the back of Loki's neck. Loki instantly dies from the bite. The pack gasps and Stella starts to cry because she lost her last protector. Midnight turns to Stella and says, "You are banished! Your bloodline has caused enough death. If you return to the pack again, I will kill you myself."

Chance screams out to his father, "No Father! You can't do that! Stella is my best friend!"

Midnight responds, "Boy, you shut your mouth. This is the best decision for you and our legacy. Never disrespect my orders again." Chance cries and runs back to the den.

Stella turns to see Chance running away and she knows now that she must leave and face the wilderness on her own. Many in the wolfpack tear up as the last of Hunter's bloodline leaves the pack for good. Stella walks off into the forest, never to see her friends again.

Chapter Seven

Stella walks for miles upon miles, days upon days. She is nervous, scared, and lonely. She is in a part of the forest that she has never seen before. She does not know what to do with her life now that she is all by herself. After walking for what seems at least a week, she starts to get immensely hungry. She had a full meal the day before she left, but now her stomach is starting to hurt. Her parents taught her very little about hunting because she was not old enough yet. She only knows from the stories that the older pups used to tell her. She decides that she wants to look for something small to get her feet on the ground. She heads into the brush looking for something small to catch. She sniffs the air and listens intently and hears something moving in the bushes.

She sees a medium-sized white rabbit coming out of the bushes a few yards away from her. She starts to walk slowly toward the rabbit from behind so it won't see her coming. The rabbit has its head down eating some grass in a field outside the edge of the bushes. She slowly approaches, and she is about five feet away and ready to pounce when she steps on a big twig. It makes a loud *crack* sound. The rabbit looks up quickly and turns around to see the wolf approaching it! The rabbit bolts into a sprint and Stella chases as fast as she can after it. The rabbit zigs and zags between the trees and Stella does her best to keep up. Stella starts to get tired because she does not have as much energy from not eating for so long. The rabbit breaks away and Stella loses it. Stella is frustrated and hungry, but she knows she must try again.

She hears the crashing of water against the shore, so she heads toward the sound to get a drink after running so hard. She bends down to get a drink and when she is done, she looks up and sees a group of beavers. She sees how big and fat they are and knows one would be delicious if she could catch it. She walks through the bushes along the edge of the lake to get closer to the beavers. The beavers are eating grass along the edge of the lake. There is a large clearing between the bushes and the beavers, so Stella knows she has to be super quiet this time. She approaches slowly after entering the clearing, making sure not to step on any twigs this time. As she gets closer, one of the beavers turns its head and sees her coming. It announces to its friends that a wolf is coming for them and they all scurry into the lake and swim away. Stella is devastated about losing another meal. She doesn't know what she is going to do about food, but she has to stop for a while and regain some energy.

Chapter Eight

Stella wakes up the next morning with her stomach throbbing. She is so frustrated that she doesn't know how to properly hunt for food. She does not know what to do. She is delirious with hunger and stares off into the distance in sorrow. She notices a group of black birds coming down from the trees and going into some pretty bushes with blue things on them. She notices the birds are eating the blue round things on the bushes. Stella thinks to herself, "If the birds are eating those, maybe I can too?"

She walks over to the bushes and scares away all of the black birds. She gathers a bunch of blue round things in her mouth and starts to chew on them. "Wow, these are delicious! I can't believe how good these taste. I think I found my source of food!" Stella bites into a bunch more blueberries, and she eats until she is full. She is so happy that now she will not starve to death.

It has been months of Stella eating berries all throughout the area. She is still alone but, there have been no threats to her as the area she is in is pretty safe. She eats as many berries as she wants and is starting to enjoy living on her own. She still has not hunted since that first day of trying because the berries have fed her well.

Stella is happily eating berries one day, minding her own business. Suddenly, she hears the footsteps of something big approaching. Stella does not know what to do and she freezes in fear. Coming out of the bushes next to her is a medium-sized black bear. Stella cowers in fear, thinking that the bear is going to kill her like the grizzly bear had killed her siblings. The bear stands on two feet and opens its arms wide. Seeing that the little wolf was scared and that there were no other wolves around, the bear eases up on its aggressive stance. The bear says to Stella, "Hey there little pup, so you are the one who is eating all of my blueberries?"

Stella was shaking in fear but responded, saying, "Yes I have. I have been so hungry. I do not know how to hunt. Please do not kill me."

"Who said I was going to kill you?"

"Another bear killed my siblings, but that bear was bigger and brown."

"Did that bear have a black tooth on the bottom of its mouth?"

"I had a brief moment of looking at the big bear before I ran, but yes, I did notice a black tooth."

"That must have been Darktooth! He is truly an evil bear. I am nothing like him."

"Yes, it does not seem like that. My name is Stella. I was the daughter of the wolf pack leader until he was killed by humans. The new leader banished me from the pack. That is why I am out here all by myself."

"Hello Stella, my name is Blackberry. I am a black bear and I love berries! Hahaha."

For the first time in a while, Stella bursts out laughing. "Oh, my dear Blackberry, that is hilarious."

"I know you are lonely and probably hungry because the berries don't always fill me up. Why don't you come with me and be my friend? I do not mind having good company. Wolves are much better at hunting than bears because you all are so much faster. Maybe I can teach you how to hunt in exchange for you catching some good food for us to eat. I don't mind helping to raise you up into a big strong wolf because no one was there to raise me into a big strong bear."

"Thank you so much Blackberry! But I don't want to be friends... I want to be BEST friends!"

"Oh, wow Stella, you scared me there for a second! Hahaha, I think this is going to be a beautiful friendship!"

The two finish eating their blueberry dinner and Blackberry says, "Let's go to my cave to take a nap. I will teach you how to hunt early tomorrow morning. I hope you are excited! I know you are going to be an amazing big wolf one day."

"Thank you, Blackberry. I look forward to your instructions."

The two walk to Blackberry's cave and sleep soundly for the rest of the day.

Chapter Nine

Stella and Blackberry wake up the next morning hungry because the blueberries are not as filling as meat. Blackberry rolls off her back and stands on her feet and stretches. She asks Stella, "Are you excited for your first hunt?"

'Of course I'm excited! I haven't had meat for so long!"

"First we will start off small and then we will work our way up to bigger animals."

"Can we catch a bunny first, and then a beaver, and then a deer? Let's say that I had a bad experience with the first two on my own," Stella tells Blackberry.

"Sure, we can do that. I have experience hunting each of those animals."

The pair leave the cave with Stella confident now that she has Blackberry's help. Blackberry leads the way out of the cave, telling Stella, "Follow me my dear. I know where the rabbits usually hang out at this time of year." They walk to a special clearing in the forest where Blackberry usually hunts for rabbits for herself.

Blackberry tells Stella, "Step one: Look around and go to a place where there are no big sticks, branches, or twigs on the ground between you and your prey." Stella nods her head in agreement. "Step two: Hunt upwind, or otherwise known as, hunt with the wind in your face."

"Why is that Blackberry?"

"So the prey does not smell you coming. Wolves have a very very strong odor!" then Blackberry grabs her nose and shakes her head. Stella laughs and shakes her head too.

"Step three: Approach, otherwise known as stalk, your prey on your tippy-toes. That way you are as quiet as possible." Stella nods her head in agreement once again.

"Step four: When you are close enough to your prey to make an attack, put all four feet firmly on the ground and lean your body weight on your back feet.

"Step five: Make the pounce when the prey is least paying attention and run as fast as you can.

"Step six: When you attack the prey, go for the neck because that is the easiest way to make the kill."

"Step seven: Eat! Stella laughs at the last step but nods her head that she has heard the instructions and knows what to do.

Blackberry moves back behind the trees so she can watch Stella from a safe distance without making noise. Stella begins to wait for a rabbit to come into the clearing before she makes her attempt. A few minutes pass by and a big brown rabbit comes into the clearing. Stella goes through the steps that Blackberry told her.

There were not any twigs on the ground between her and the bunny. Next, the wind was blowing in Stella's face. Then, the bunny has its back turned to Stella so she approaches on her tippy-toes. Next, Stella is in position so she puts her feet on the ground and leans back on her hind legs. Then Stella pounces! She runs at full speed and before the rabbit can react she is close enough to catch it before it runs too far away. She tackles it with her two front paws and bites down firmly on its neck. The rabbit stops moving and dies in Stella's jaws.

Stella brings her first kill over to where Blackberry was watching. Blackberry says, "For your first successful hunt, that wasn't bad at all." Stella and Blackberry split the rabbit between them and enjoy a wonderful meal of meat.

The next day, Stella attempts to hunt for the second time. This time, Stella is going to catch a beaver. She is nervous because the last time she tried to catch a beaver it went so poorly, but now that she has Blackberry's help she knows she can do it. The pair go to the edge of a river where Blackberry usually hunts for large beavers. Blackberry reminds Stella of the seven steps before she sends Stella out to hunt.

Stella sees a group of large beavers along the river eating leaves from shrubs. "Step One," Stella thinks to herself. She remembers that she has to find a location without large twigs and sticks on the ground between her and the beavers. Next, she maneuvers herself upwind so the beavers can't smell her. She approaches her prey on tippy toes and gets in position to attack. She puts her four paws on the ground and prepares herself for the pounce. When the beavers were deep in conversation with each other, not paying attention, Stella attacks. She goes for the largest, fattest, and slowest beaver. The beavers all scatter but Stella's prey is too slow, and she catches it before it jumps in the river and swims away. She goes for the neck and makes a successful kill. Blackberry comes from the forest after watching her and she cheers. "Yay Stella! You did it again! Congratulations! You are getting so much better."

"Thank you but I could not have done this without you."

"Let's eat!" The two chow down on their nice meal and it fills them up for a few hours.

The next day is the final test for Stella. They go on the hunt for a blacktail deer. Blackberry has never been fast enough to catch a deer herself, but she has confidence that the young wolf will be able to catch one. "No matter what happens today, you will always be a winner in my eyes. Just be confident in yourself. I believe in you."

"Thank you, I will try my best."

They walk through the forest for a few hours looking for a deer. In the distance, Stella sees what they are looking for. She whispers to Blackberry, "Look, there is a deer right there."

Blackberry whispers back, "Go get it Stella, remember the steps."

Stella stalks the deer very slowly. She approaches on a path with no twigs or sticks on the ground, but nice, soft, quiet grass. She moves around upwind. She approaches on her tippy toes. Hiding behind a tree, she gets close enough to approach from behind while the deer is not paying attention. She sits flat on all four paws and prepares for the attack. When she thinks the deer is most vulnerable, she pounces! She gets close before the deer reacts, but the deer escapes her first jump. She pursues the deer through the trees and gains ground. When the deer tries to cut to the left it trips and falls on the ground. Stella is right behind it and pounces on top and bites for the neck. The deer struggles for a few seconds but succumbs to Stella's assault. Stella has officially caught her first deer. Blackberry comes running up through the trees to see if Stella caught the deer. When she saw the deer on the ground, she rose up on two paws and cheered loudly. "Wow!! You did it! That was so amazing! I am so proud of you Stella!"

"I am proud of myself too. I didn't think I could do it either, but I overcame my fears and I just did it!"

"You know what I am going to say next! Step seven! Let's eat!"

The two have a wondrous feast of deer that made them full for the next three days. They celebrate for the next two weeks for Stella's first successful deer hunt. The two team up and hunt every day going forward. With Blackberry's strength and Stella's cunning and speed, they can catch almost anything.

Chapter Ten

The pair spend the next few years in the Alaskan forests enjoying life and growing stronger. Stella has grown into a full-sized adult wolf. She is big, she is strong, she is smart, she is confident, and she is AWESOME!

Stella and Blackberry were looking for their favorite snack one afternoon, blueberries! They were rummaging through their favorite bushes eating up all the blueberries they could find. They hadn't a care in the world and were not paying attention to their surroundings at all. In this part of the forest, they were the big dogs. Nobody messed with them.

As they were rummaging, Stella hears a twig break nearby. She does not think anything of it and continues to munch on her berries with Blackberry. Then, out of nowhere, a giant figure appears through the trees running at them. Stella looks up in fear and sees it is a grizzly bear! It opens its mouth wide and she saw the same dark tooth she had seen when she was a pup. Blackberry turns when she hears the roar and sees that it is Darktooth. "Darktooth, stop! Get out of here or else!"

"What can you do to stop me Blackberry? I recognize the smell of that wolf. I remember that I killed her family years ago. I am here to finish what I started."

Stella shakes in fear, as her childhood nightmare comes back to life. She is too afraid to defend herself.

Blackberry roars, "You will have to go through me to get to her. Try your best you evil creature!"

Darktooth charges at Blackberry. The two begin a tremendous battle. They claw and bite each other ferociously. Darktooth's greater size and strength eventually overcomes Blackberry and she collapses to the ground, too hurt to continue the battle. Darktooth turns away from Blackberry after conquering his foe. "Time to die little pup!" He approaches Stella with blood on his lips and a smile on his face. Stella is too scared to move. Just before Darktooth jumps onto Stella, a huge figure jumps out of the bushes.

It is a giant grey wolf that pounces from the bushes onto Darktooth, knocking him down. The wolf is ferocious and strong. He fights with Darktooth for several minutes. They claw and bite each other, trying to gain the upper hand. Darktooth goes for the kill and tries to bite down on the mysterious wolf, but he misses and exposes his neck. The wolf turns his head quickly, seeing the opening. He goes for the counter attack and makes the killing bite on Darktooth. The giant grizzly bear collapses on the ground, defeated by the wolf. Stella is still too afraid to move, but the wolf comes up to her, bloody and bruised. Stella looks deep into the wolf's eyes and says, "Aaron?"

Chapter Eleven

"Stella? Is that you?"

"Yes, it is me! You saved my life! I thought you were dead!"

"No! The bear did not kill me. I have been looking for him and you for all these years to avenge the death of my siblings." They embrace. Stella goes to check on Blackberry.

"Blackberry are you okay? I can't believe you fought Darktooth for me!"

"I am okay. A little sore and bleeding but I am okay."

"Blackberry, this is my brother Aaron."

"Hello Aaron, I have heard so much about you!"

Aaron responds, "Thank you for protecting my sister. Now let's all get some rest and talk when we recover."

The next day Stella wakes up and sees her brother sleeping on the floor next to her. She is happy beyond words. Aaron and Blackberry hear Stella moving around and they wake up. "Good morning sister," Aaron says.

"Good morning brother! We have so much to talk about."

"Why aren't you with the pack? I have been hunting for Darktooth for years, but when I caught both your scent and his, I was totally confused."

"The pack went on a hunt one day and human hunters shot both of our parents. They did not survive."

Aaron puts his head down and starts to cry. "I can't believe they are dead. But that doesn't explain why you are here in the wild. What happened?"

"Midnight seized the throne. The pack went on another hunt and the human hunters came back. This time no one died, but Midnight was angry. He thought

44

that our bloodline was the cause of the attacks, so he kicked me out of the pack. Loki tried to stand up for me and fought Midnight, but Midnight killed him."

Aaron turns from sorrow to rage! "What!?! How dare he defame our parents and our bloodline. How dare he banish you to the wild! How dare he kill Loki! I swear on this day that I will have my revenge, in my mother's and father's name! Do you know where the pack is? They were not where they always were when I looked for them."

Stella is surprised the pack has moved. "Wow, I don't understand why they would leave our ancestral home, something else Midnight did to break tradition. I have no idea where they are, but I will be glad to help you find them! Are you coming Blackberry?"

"I wouldn't miss this for the world! We are sisters in blood now!"

Chapter Twelve

The trio search for six weeks. One day on a foggy morning, they turn from a clearing into a canyon ravine. Aaron yells out, "Everyone stop! I smell something familiar." Stella and Blackberry freeze. Aaron takes a few more steps in the direction of the smell and says, "We found them!" He starts to walk quickly, following the scent with Stella and Blackberry close on his tail. After a few miles of searching, they come into a clearing and see the pack of wolves lying in the sunlight that just broke through the fog.

As Aaron, Stella, and Blackberry approach, they see a large wolf standing at the edge of the pack circle waiting for them. It is Midnight. He yells out to the three, "Halt! Stop where you are! I knew I recognized that scent." The three don't stop and the pack is all stirring from their rest and look up to see the two wolves and the bear approaching.

Aaron walks within ten yards of Midnight and yells out, "I am here to reclaim the throne and avenge the death of Loki. I challenge you to a fight to the death!"

The Elders get between both Midnight and Aaron and declare, "Aaron is alive, and he has a right to claim the throne. A formal battle must take place to see who will be pack leader. Pack, prepare for the battle!"

The pack gets in a giant circle with Aaron and Midnight on opposite sides. Stella and Blackberry wait anxiously for the fight to begin. Stella goes up to Aaron just before the fight starts and tells him, "Do it for our bloodline." Aaron nods his head and turns back to Midnight.

The Elders declare the fight has begun and Midnight and Aaron charge after each other. The fight is brutal. Both wolves are determined to kill the other.

They are of equal size and equal ferocity. They claw, bite, and attack each other with no mercy. The fight is even for several minutes until Aaron makes a mistake and leaves himself open for a counter attack. Midnight knocks him over and claws his face, knocking dirt into his eyes. Aaron is blind and can't see. Midnight stands over the top of him and yells out, "Now the Hunter bloodline will be gone forever." Just as Midnight is about to bite down and finish off Aaron, his son Chance comes running out of the pack circle.

Chance yells, "Stop, Father! Let them go or else!!"

Midnight responds in anger, "What are you going to do to me? You can't stop me!"

Chance responds, "You banished the love of my life and I am here to avenge her!"

Chance jumps at his father and knocks him away from Aaron. Another ferocious battle ensues. They fight back and forth and tear flesh from each other's bodies.

Midnight is growing weak from the two battles and

Chance is gaining momentum. In Midnight's fatigue, he

makes a poor lunge and leaves himself open for attack.

Chance takes the opportunity and bites at his father.

Midnight yells out in pain as Chance puts on a death

grip on his neck. After a few seconds of struggling,

Midnight is vanquished.

Chapter Thirteen

Chance leaves his dead father on the ground to go check on Aaron. Stella runs up to Aaron on the ground as well. The dirt in Aaron's eyes has been washed away by his natural tears and he gets up off the ground. He looks at Chance and says, "Thank you Chance for saving my life. I owe you the world. The only thing I can think of giving you in repayment is this: I relinquish my claim to the throne to you on one condition. You must marry my sister and keep our bloodline as rulers of the pack for the rest of time."

Aaron smiles and responds, "I would love that, but it is up to your sister if she wants to marry me."

Aaron and Chance both look at Stella and she says, "Yes! Of course!"

Chance runs over to Stella and they embrace each other. Stella says, "I missed you so much!"

"I missed you too my love! Let's get married and start our own dynasty."

The next day the pack gathers early in the morning. The Elders go to the middle of the pack circle and call Stella and Aaron to come to the middle. "We are gathered here today to wed Chance and Stella together. They will be wed as leaders of our pack for the rest of their lives. Everyone bow you heads and howl if you approve of this wedding." The entire pack howls and Blackberry even joins in and does a bear growl. Everyone lifts their heads and the Elders say, "I now pronounce you two husband and wife. You may kiss to seal the covenant." Stella and Chance kiss and embrace. The entire pack howls with happiness and tears flow down their faces. Blackberry roars with even more tears coming down her face. After a long, hard, scary, and painful trial, the wild journey of the young wolf Stella is now over.